Sly the Sleuth

and the Food Mysteries

by Donna Jo Napoli and Robert Furrow

illustrated by Heather Maione

Dial Books for Young Readers

DIAL BOOKS FOR YOUNG READERS
A division of Penguin Young Readers Group
Published by The Penguin Group
Penguin Group (USA) Inc., 375 Hudson Street, New York, NY 10014, U.S.A.
Penguin Group (Canada), 90 Eglinton Avenue East, Suite 700, Toronto, Ontario, Canada
M4P 2Y3 (a division of Pearson Penguin Canada Inc.)
Penguin Books Ltd, 80 Strand, London WC2R 0RL, England
Penguin Ireland, 25 St. Stephen's Green, Dublin 2, Ireland
(a division of Penguin Books Ltd)
Penguin Group (Australia), 250 Camberwell Road, Camberwell, Victoria 3124, Australia
(a division of Pearson Australia Group Pty Ltd)
Penguin Books India Pvt Ltd, 11 Community Centre,
Panchsheel Park, New Delhi - 110 017, India
Penguin Group (NZ), Cnr Airborne and Rosedale Roads, Albany, Auckland 1310,
New Zealand (a division of Pearson New Zealand Ltd)
Penguin Books (South Africa) (Pty) Ltd, 24 Sturdee Avenue, Rosebank,
Johannesburg 2196, South Africa
Penguin Books Ltd, Registered Offices: 80 Strand, London WC2R 0RL, England

Text copyright © 2007 by Donna Jo Napoli and Robert Furrow
Illustrations copyright © 2007 by Heather Maione
The publisher does not have any control over and does not assume any
responsibility for author or third-party websites or their content.
Designed by Jasmin Rubero
Text set in Bembo
Printed in the U.S.A.
1   3   5   7   9   10   8   6   4   2
Library of Congress Cataloging-in-Publication Data
Napoli, Donna Jo, date.
Sly the sleuth and the food mysteries / by Donna Jo Napoli and
Robert Furrow ; illustrated by Heather Maione.
        p.   cm.
Summary: Sly uses her detective skills to help her friends solve the
case of something fishy, something cooking, and something seedy.
ISBN-13: 978-0-8037-3119-6
[1. Food—Fiction. 2. Friendship—Fiction. 3. Mystery and detective stories.]
I. Furrow, Robert, date. II. Maione, Heather Harms, ill. III. Title.
PZ7.N15Skq 2007
[Fic]—dc22
2006008167

*Thanks to our family,
and Rebecca Waugh and Lauri Hornik,
(and Taxi, of course)
—D.J.N and R.F.*

*For Bob, who thankfully understands that
cooking has always been a mystery to me
—H.M.*

Case #1:

Sly and Something Fishy

Slow Season

I kneeled on the floor by my sign. In black letters I wrote: SLEUTH FOR HIRE. That is the name of my agency.

I looked at it hard. My father says ads should catch the eye. They should be bold. My sign was not bold.

Brian was beside me. He was working on his picture of a T. rex. Brian is my neighbor. He's only four. But he can be good company. Sometimes.

Brian's T. rex was orange and blue and lime. With purple stripes.

He added a giant tooth. In red.

It was bold.

"Can I borrow your red crayon?" I asked.

Brian put his finger in his mouth. He handed me the red crayon.

It had no tip. Neither did his other crayons. And this was a new pack.

"Brian, you press too hard."

Brian mumbled. I couldn't understand. His finger was still in his mouth.

"Why's your finger in your mouth?" I asked.

Brian pulled his finger out. He wiped it on his sleeve. "Are you putting hearts on it?" he asked.

"You mean my sign?"

"Red is good for hearts," said Brian.

"Why would I put hearts on my sign?"

Brian laughed. "For love."

"What? This is advertising. I need business."
I hadn't had a new case in weeks. Winter must
be the slow season for sleuths.

"Love is good for business." Brian made a
green squiggle on the corner of my sign.

"What's that?"

"Frogs are good for business too."

That was a frog? But it looked sort of cute.

I printed red words under the black ones
that were already there:

NO PROBLEM TOO SMALL
REASONABLE PRICES

The letters were fat, because the crayon had
no tip.

But my sign was bold now.

I added hearts.

A little love never hurts.

Too Much Work

I sat on my heels and watched. Brian made a border of frogs on my sign.

"Wilson," he said. Wilson is what Brian calls his frogs. All his frogs. He has dozens.

I liked it.

Bang!

"Jack!" screamed Brian.

I knew what he meant. In the fall Jack had banged his soccer ball on my door.

"That's no soccer ball," I said. "It's too cold for soccer balls."

Bang!

Brian ran to the door. He opened it. "Jack!"

Jack tucked his ball under his arm. He came in.

Brian didn't say "I told you so."

But I was annoyed anyway. I don't like being wrong. "I told you before," I said to Jack. "I prefer knocking."

"Knocking schmocking," said Jack.

"What's that mean?" asked Brian.

"Soccer balls are better than knocking," said Jack. "Hey, nice T. rex."

"He bites," said Brian.

Jack jumped. "Grrr!" He showed his teeth.

Brian screamed. He ran behind me.

"What about my sign?" I said.

Jack frowned. "It looks like Christmas. Christmas is past."

Brian peeked out. "What makes it Christmas?"

"Red and green."

Brian frowned.

My sign did look Christmas-y.

I frowned now. This was my only piece of poster board. And it was already used on the other side. "What are you doing here, Jack?"

"I have a case for you. About Fluffy."

Fluffy is Jack's cat. She also happens to be Kate's cat. But Kate calls her Clarissa. And she happens to be a woman named Julie's cat. But Julie calls her Punky. They all share her.

Knock knock knock.

Melody came in. She's my best friend. She knocks. But she never waits for me to open the door.

"I have a case for you," said Melody.

"I already hired her," said Jack.

"I'm not hired till I accept," I said. "I don't even know what your case is, Jack."

"My case is important," said Melody. "It's dangerous."

"Danger!" screamed Brian.

"I was here first," said Jack.

"Two cases at once," I said. "Let me think."

Priorities

"Yay!" shouted Brian. "Christmas worked."

"What?" said Melody.

I pointed at my sign. "He means my sign worked. And I haven't even put it in the front yard yet."

"I wanted to hire you before I saw your sign," said Jack.

"I did too," said Melody.

"See?" said Brian. "Magic."

"Oh yeah?" Jack touched the corner of my sign with his sneaker. "Whose case are you taking, Sly?"

This was tough.

Jack had brought me two cases in the past. One was about Wish Fish, his Siamese fighting fish. The other was about soccer.

Melody had brought me two cases in the past. One was about Pong, her puppy. The other was about kicking.

They were both good clients.

I have two policies. First, I take only cases that are fun. Second, I take only cases a cat would care about. After all, my cat Taxi listens to me talk about cases. I don't want to bore her.

Taxi would like a case about Fluffy-Clarissa-Punky. Probably any cat would.

But Melody was my best friend. And danger should take priority. Plus, Taxi likes Melody.

"I'll take both," I said. "But Melody's first."

Fishy

"No fair," said Jack. "I . . ." He stopped and looked at Melody. His face turned pink and sappy. "All right. But solve Melody's fast."

This was a disturbing order. What if Melody's case was hard? "Cases take as long as cases take," I said. That sounded official.

"You have one week," said Jack. "My cousins are coming Friday." He dribbled his ball to the door. "We want to play shuffleboard." He went out.

Brian ran to the door. He shouted, "I want to play shuffleboard."

"Great idea," Jack shouted back. "I'll see you Friday."

Jack wanted Brian to come play shuffle-board? Brian?

Something fishy was going on.

"Shut the door, Brian," said Melody. "The cold is coming in."

Brian shut the door.

I turned to Melody. "Start at the beginning." That was sleuth talk.

"I can't tell with you-know-who here." Melody jerked her head toward Brian.

"Time to go, Brian." I collected his crayons. It wasn't fair to send him home so fast. He'd come only a little while ago. But business was business.

Brian rolled up his T. rex picture. He didn't even argue.

This was fishier than Jack inviting Brian for shuffleboard. "Are you feeling okay?" I asked.

"No." Brian stuck his finger in his mouth. He moved it around in there.

"What's wrong?"

Brian dropped his hand. "I can't tell you."

Brian told everyone everything. Something might really be wrong. Or maybe he was just echoing Melody.

I handed Brian his crayons.

He left.

"Why couldn't you talk in front of Brian?"

"It's scary," said Melody.

Something dangerous and scary. I wasn't sure I wanted this case, after all. But I owed Melody a try. "What's scary?"

"See for yourself. Come home with me."

Bushes

I followed Melody across Brian's backyard. We ducked through the hedge into her yard.

Bushes run along the front of Melody's house. She stopped and held aside branches. "Look."

I peeked past her arm. "I don't see anything."

"Look down."

It was dark back there. But I spied trash. A candy wrapper. A potato chip bag. Stuff like that.

Nothing dangerous or scary.

"See?" said Melody. She was excited.

"Trash," I said as nicely as I could.

"Exactly," said Melody.

This case was going nowhere. I cleared my throat. "Why did you throw trash behind your bush?"

"Don't be dumb," said Melody. "I didn't do it."

"Who did?"

"That's the mystery. Someone's living in our bushes."

"Have you seen him?"

"No," said Melody. "He hides when I come."

"How do you know?"

"He isn't here now," said Melody.

There was something wrong with that logic. But I let it go. What mattered was that Melody was afraid. "If he hides when you come, he can't be very scary."

"Unless he's waiting for the right moment," said Melody. "Then he'll do something awful."

"Maybe no one's living here. Maybe someone's just throwing trash behind the bushes."

"Find out," said Melody. "Because if someone's living here, he's dangerous."

Melody liked to be dramatic.

But she could be right.

Pong

I pushed my way through. The branches poked my tummy and chest. They pinned me to the house. So I squatted.

Near the base of the bush there was more room. But not much.

I gathered the trash. The potato chip bag was half full. And there was one piece of toffee left in the candy wrapper. I stuffed everything in my pocket.

"What are you doing?" called Melody from the other side of the bushes.

"Gathering clues."

"What did you find?"

"Trash."

"I know that," said Melody. "What else?"

"Give me time." I felt around.

The leaves between this bush and the next were broken off at the bottom. I crawled under the broken leaves. It was like a tunnel.

It scraped at my back. I wound up out on the front lawn.

I stood beside Melody. It would be hard for anyone my size to go through that tunnel. But it wouldn't be hard for a dog. "Did Pong discover the trash?"

"How did you know?"

"It's my job." I liked saying that. It sounded sleuthy. "Go get Pong."

"What? Are you going to interrogate him?" Melody giggled.

"Just get him, okay?"

Melody went inside. She came out with Pong.

Pong yipped happily and ran at me.

I roughhoused with him. He likes that. Then I sat on my heels.

Pong sniffed at my pocket.

"Aha!" I pulled out the potato chip bag. I offered Pong a chip.

He ate it.

"Aha! Pong likes potato chips."

"All dogs do," said Melody. "So what?"

I thought of offering Pong the toffee. But toffee is sticky. Pong probably couldn't chew it right. "Does he like candy too?"

"Yesterday he came out with a Rice Krispies Treat in his mouth. He swallowed it before I could stop him."

"Aha!" I said. "Pong knew there was trash behind your bush. Maybe Pong put it there. Maybe he eats trash there."

"Pong eats anything he finds," said Melody.

"And he doesn't go behind things to do it. He's too young to know he shouldn't eat junk. Besides, where would Pong get all that stuff?"

"Good points. But whoever left that trash back there was skinny," I said. "And short."

Melody looked surprised. Then she laughed. "Are you saying someone Pong's height did it? A leprechaun?"

Melody's Irish. Her leprechaun jokes crack me up. A leprechaun eating junk food—I laughed too.

Interruptions

After dinner I went to my room. I spread the clues on my desk. They didn't look like the sort of thing someone dangerous would eat. They looked like the sort of thing a kid would eat.

The phone rang.

My mother called up the stairs, "Sly, it's Jack."

I walked to the hall phone. "Hi, Jack."

"Did you solve Melody's case yet?"

"Don't rush me."

"I have to," said Jack. "My cousins love shuffle-board. And remind Brian to bring cookies. I just called and told him. But you remind him too."

Jack wanted Brian to bring cookies? Brian's cookies were made by his mother. Mrs. Olsen was a health nut. And her cookies tasted like it. No one liked them.

Oh! Now I remembered.

"Are you still using Brian's mother's cookies as pucks?"

"They're the best. Hurry." Jack hung up.

So that's why Jack invited Brian. Good. I had figured out one thing.

Now if I could only figure out who put trash behind Melody's bushes.

I walked toward my room. Uh-oh. Another interruption.

Brian was standing at the top of the stairs. He held a cookie tin. "Take these."

"Jack asked for them, not me."

"Keep them till Friday," said Brian.

"You keep them."

"No. My mom will want me to eat more. They make me sick."

I almost laughed. That's how I felt about Brian's mother's cookies too. But it wasn't nice to say it. "Okay." I put the cookie tin on the floor in the corner.

When I turned around, Brian was already halfway down the stairs.

I felt sorry for him. Little kids should be happy when their mothers make cookies. "Hey," I called. "We've got cookies too. Come into the kitchen."

"No," said Brian.

"No?" I ran down. "Why not?"

"My mother already made me eat some of hers." Brian stuck his finger in his mouth and dug around. It came out with brown gunk under the nail. He wiped it off on his pajama top.

"Yuck, Brian. What was that?"

"I can't tell you."

Rot

"Brian, you tell me everything."

Brian's eyes filled with tears.

I took his hand. We went into the kitchen. When I'm sad, my mother gives me fruit and a glass of milk. Then we talk.

Brian isn't a fruit fiend, like me. I poured him milk. "We had chicken for dinner. My father's famous chicken. The leftovers are still warm. Want a piece?"

"I'm not hungry."

This was odd. Brian loved our chicken. "Not even a drumstick?" Drumsticks are my favorite. I put a drumstick on a plate.

Brian took a bite. He spit it out. His face crumpled. He was really crying now.

"Start at the beginning," I said, even though this wasn't a case. The beginning is the right place, no matter what.

"Promise you won't tell."

This was a dilemma. I keep my promises. "Is it a big problem, Brian?"

"Yes."

"Then your mom should know."

"It'll make her sad."

"Why?"

"She thinks they're good," said Brian.

"She thinks what's good?"

"And she doesn't want me to rot." Brian's tears were big.

I put my arms around Brian. "What are you talking about?"

"Teeth."

"Drink your milk," I said. "Milk's good for teeth."

"Milk stinks." Brian wrinkled his nose. "Your father's famous chicken stinks. Everything stinks after dinner."

"Everything stinks after dinner?"

Brian's face pinched with fear. "Everything."

"Let me see your nose."

Brian tilted his head up.

There was nothing strange about Brian's nose.

"Open your mouth."

Brian opened his mouth.

His breath stank. Like dead fish.

Fluffy

I sat at my desk and stared at Melody's trash. I didn't care about her case anymore.

Brian had a problem. And it was making him sad. And scared. More scared than Melody was about this trash.

I went out in the hall to the telephone. I looked at it.

Brian didn't want me to call his mother.

But I hadn't actually promised not to.

I put my hand on the telephone. Then I dropped it.

I went back to my room.

The cookie tin sat in the corner. It was like a big finger pointing at me. Telling me that Brian needed my help.

I went back to the telephone. I called Jack.

"Hello."

"Hi, Jack. Come get your shuffleboard pucks."

"Brian's mom made cookies already?"

"Come get them. I don't want them here. And you better be nice to Brian on Friday. He's coming to your house to play shuffleboard."

"I'm always nice to Brian," said Jack.

That was true. Jack was a good guy. I had only said that about being nice because I was upset.

"But I can't come get the cookies," said Jack.

"Why not?"

"Fluffy will eat them before we get a chance to play shuffleboard."

"Cats don't eat cookies," I said.

But Jack had already hung up.

Fish

"I'm going next door," I said to my mother.

"At this hour? Brian is asleep. It's nearly your bedtime, Sly."

"I'm going to talk with Mrs. Olsen. Besides, it's Saturday. It's okay if I'm up later. And it's for a case."

"All right then."

I rang Brian's doorbell.

The light over the steps went on.

Mrs. Olsen's face peeked around the curtain covering the glass in the door. She looked worried. Then she smiled. She opened the door.

"Hello, Sly. Brian's in bed."

"I came to talk to you."

"How nice. Would you like a snack?"

"I don't eat before bed." This was one time I was grateful for my mother's rules. "Thanks anyway."

We went into the living room and sat on the couch.

"Mrs. Olsen, did Brian have fish for dinner?"

"No. He hates fish. I never cook it."

"Do you have any idea why his breath might smell like fish?"

Mrs. Olsen looked aghast. "Does his breath smell like fish?"

"Yes."

"When did you smell it?"

"Tonight. When he came over."

"Oh, dear." Mrs. Olsen put her hand to her mouth. "I guess I overdid it with that last batch."

"Excuse me?"

Mrs. Olsen patted my knee. "I add fish oil to cakes and cookies." She gave a little smile. "It makes them more nutritious. That way I don't feel guilty about giving Brian sweets. You'd never know it, of course. The taste is hardly there."

That's what you think, I thought.

"Well, last week I read about a new concentrated fish oil. It's wonderful for you. So I bought a bottle. I used it in this week's cookies. Brian always gets cookies after dinner, you know. But if his mouth smells like fish, this oil is too strong."

Brian eats fishy cookies every night. The poor kid.

"Oh my," muttered Mrs. Olsen. "I thought his enthusiasm for cookies had dropped off. Oh my."

"Treats are treats," I said. "They're not supposed to be good for you. They're supposed to taste good."

Mrs. Olsen put her hands together in her lap. "Well, Sly, treats can be both. I just made a little mistake buying this new oil."

I don't like arguing with adults. And Mrs. Olsen was proud of her cooking. But this was Brian we were talking about. I looked at Mrs. Olsen hard. "Treats shouldn't taste like fish. Not even a little bit."

Mrs. Olsen glanced away. "You know," she said at last, "I can use olive oil from now on. Olive oil is good for you. It tastes good too. Yes. I'll make a new batch of cookies tomorrow."

Warm relief filled me. And I hadn't broken Brian's trust. Sometimes things just went right. "I bet he'll love them."

"If he loves my sweets too much, I'll have to make sure he brushes extra good." Mrs. Olsen smiled. "We can't have rotten teeth now, can we?"

Rotten teeth.

Brian had said his mother didn't want him to rot. When I'd asked what he was talking about, he said teeth. But that didn't make sense: Fish oil won't rot your teeth. But junk food might.

Melody's Bushes

After brunch on Sunday I sneaked behind our garage. I watched the hedge between Brian's backyard and Melody's backyard.

I waited.

Nothing happened.

I waited some more.

Brian ran out his back door. He cut through the hedge.

I knew he would.

I followed him.

He went around the front of Melody's house. And disappeared.

I crawled through the little tunnel between the bushes. Branches poked me hard. But I gritted my teeth; this was important.

"Hi, Brian," I said.

"Hi, Sly." He moved over and I squished in. "Want candy?" He slapped something in my hand.

"Sure." I took a bite. It was a Hershey's bar. "This is good."

"I know," said Brian.

"Things taste good in the morning?" I asked.

"I have popcorn too."

"Your mom doesn't know about this, does she? That's why you're hiding, right?"

"Candy makes her sad," said Brian.

Hmmm. I wondered if Mrs. Olsen had ever tried chocolate. Chocolate makes my mother happy.

"Where did you get this junk food, Brian?"

"I traded at school."

"What did you trade?" I asked.

"Toys."

That sounded bad. "How many toys have you traded?"

"Lots."

Oops. Brian needed his toys. Any kid did. "Did you start trading because your mother's cookies suddenly tasted bad?"

"They made Mitchell sick too," said Brian. Mitchell goes to Brian's nursery.

"Is that why you think your teeth are rotting? Because of the candy?"

"Have more," said Brian. He slapped some in my hand.

I ate it and licked my fingers. "Well, you don't have to trade anymore."

"I like candy," said Brian. "Better than home cookies."

I took Brian's hand. "Listen. Your mom's cookies are going to taste better from now on. Better than ever. You won't need junk food."

"Junk food is good," said Brian.

"For treats now and then," I said. "You have to watch out for some candy, though."

"Toffee," said Brian.

"Exactly," I said. "It sticks in your teeth."

"Rotten teeth." Brian's voice was sober.

"Brushing works," I said.

I heard a rip. The smell of popcorn was strong. Brian chewed loudly.

Three birds

I told Melody Brian was the dangerous guy in the bushes. She laughed. And she gave me two poster boards as payment. They're both used on one side. But the other side is good for signs, if I need more later.

And I might. Because I already solved Jack's case. His problem was that Fluffy-Clarissa-Punky kept eating the shuffleboard pucks. That was so easy to solve, I didn't charge him. I explained that she liked the fish oil in them. So, once his cat has eaten up all the fishy cookie-pucks, he has two choices. He can buy regular pucks. The kind made of plastic. Like normal people use. Or he can ask Brian for more cookies—the new kind without fish oil.

Jack never has extra money. So he's decided to ask Brian to play shuffleboard often. And to bring cookies each time.

That will make Mrs. Olsen happy. So long as she never finds out what the cookies are used for.

And Brian is happy. He says home cookies taste good again. Better than ever, like I promised. Poor Brian. He'll never understand what a really good cookie tastes like. But at least he's happy. And he doesn't have to worry about rotting teeth. Plus Melody and I gave him old toys, to replace the ones he traded away.

Taxi got a bonus out of all of this. I took some of the fishy cookies from Jack's stash. I gave her one. And I told her about this case. She gnawed and purred the whole time I talked.

So everyone's problems were related. My father says it's like hitting two birds with one stone. But it was really three birds.

Actually, it was three fish. Ha. I was right: There was something fishy about how Jack and Brian were acting. Ha.

I'm glad when cases end up funny like that.

Case #2:
Sly and Something Cooking

T-shirts

It was Friday. On Friday cheerleading practice met at my house. I hurried home to clean up before the others got there.

Brian was waiting by my back door. He had both arms squeezed around Taxi.

"Taxi doesn't like to be held," I said.

"I have a present for her." Brian followed me inside. He put Taxi down. He took off his backpack. Then he took off his jacket. "Look, Sly. Look at my shirt."

His T-shirt had MASCOT printed on it in Magic Marker.

Kate was the captain of the squad. That's because the whole idea of the squad was hers. When Brian asked to be a cheerleader, Kate had said no. But she'd made him mascot, instead. Kate can be nice when she isn't being bossy.

"I've seen your mascot shirt a million times, Brian."

"Good." Brian unzipped his backpack. He held up a baby T-shirt. On it was printed MASCAT.

I stared. Brian practiced his letters at my house. I knew his handwriting. Brian had printed those letters.

"It's for Taxi," said Brian. "Get it?"

I still stared.

"Laugh. My mom laughed." Brian grabbed Taxi again. "Help me put it on her."

I shook my head in amazement. But I put the shirt over Taxi's head. I fit her front legs through the armholes. It hung on her all crazy and baggy. "Brian, did you think of this your-self? When did you learn how to spell *cat*?"

"*Cat* is in the *at* family," said Brian. "With *bat* and *fat* and *sat*. Don't you know the *at* family, Sly? I can teach you. It's easy."

My mother had said Brian was brilliant. Maybe she was right. I wasn't sure I liked the idea of having a genius neighbor. "It's a great shirt, Brian."

Knock knock knock. Melody and Princess came in.

Brian held Taxi up. "Look."

"Meow." Taxi squirmed free. She ran off.

"Wow," said Melody.

"Cool," said Princess. "Will Taxi wear it to basketball games?"

"Do you have a cat, Princess?" I asked.

"No," said Princess.

I didn't think so. "Cats can't go to games."

Knock knock.

I opened the door.

Kate stood there. "Cheerleading is over," she said.

Recipes

"How can practice be over already?" said Melody. "We haven't started yet."

"It's over." Kate opened the tote bag on her shoulder. She handed out envelopes.

"What's this?" asked Melody.

"Recipes."

"How come?" I asked.

"We're going to cook together."

"I love cooking," said Princess. She opened her envelope and took out the paper inside. "Oh, no." Princess stared at her recipe.

"You're not supposed to say 'Oh, no,'" said Kate. "You're supposed to say 'Good.'"

"Spaghetti with oil and garlic," read Melody from her own recipe. "Is that good?"

"Ask Princess," said Kate.

"Why should she ask me?" said Princess.

"It's an Italian recipe. They all are. And you're Italian."

"I'm American. My father's Italian."

"Picky, picky," said Kate.

"Since when do cheerleaders cook?" I asked.

"We're not cheerleaders," said Kate. "Not anymore."

"I like being on the squad," said Princess.

"A minute ago you said you love to cook," said Kate.

"I like being on the squad better," said Princess.

"Don't make trouble, Princess," said Kate. "I hurt my ankle, so there is no more squad."

"You can't just do that," said Melody. "We'll wait for your ankle to heal."

"I hate waiting. Now we're a cooking club. We can be on TV."

"TV?" I put my hand on Kate's forehead. "Are you delirious?"

Kate brushed my hand away. "Don't you know about the cooking channels?"

"But those aren't ordinary people," I said.

"My cousin's on TV." Kate put her hands on her hips. "And he's ordinary. He's totally ordinary."

"Really?" asked Melody.

"Well, no. He's my second cousin. Removed once or twice. But he has a cooking show. So when I write to him about our club, we can be on his show."

"Why do you even want to be on TV?" I asked.

"Everyone wants to be on TV."

Brian pulled on Kate's shirt. "I'm still mascot, right?"

"Cooking clubs don't have mascots," said Kate.

Brian shut his mouth. His chin trembled.

"Melody's right," I said. "You can't just do that, Kate."

"Yes I can. I started the squad. I can end it."

"But Brian is mascot. And Taxi is mascat. Brian made her a T-shirt."

"Mascat?" Kate gave a lopsided smile. "That's cute. Show me the shirt."

"Taxi ran away," said Brian.

"But it's a good-looking shirt," I said.

"Okay," said Kate. "Our cooking club can have a mascot and a mascat. The TV cameras will love that."

"Can I keep my pom-poms?" asked Brian.

"Sure."

"Yay!"

Brian's Contribution

"We'll do everything just like with cheerleading," said Kate. "On Monday we'll cook at my house. Tuesday will be off, because of Melody's ballet lessons. On Wednesday we'll cook at Melody's house. On Thursday we'll cook at Princess's house. And on Friday we'll cook at Sly's house. We'll share on buying ingredients. And the person whose house we're at has to make sure we have all the measuring cups and things. That way we can do it right."

"Who said we even want to do it at all?" I asked.

Kate put her fists on her hips. "I know you like to cook, Sly."

That was true. I like cooking. But it's important to stand up to Kate. I was about to say I didn't like my recipe. Then I looked at it. Linguine with pesto. That dish was yummy. I cleared my throat. "How come you get to pick the recipes?"

"It's my club." Kate took off her jacket. "Let's start."

"Whoa," I said. "Nobody brought ingredients. And I don't have all this stuff."

"We have ingredients at my house," said Brian.

"I've heard about your mother," said Kate. "You have only weird health food ingredients."

That was a low blow. I put my arm around Brian's shoulders.

But he jumped away. He opened his backpack. "Here." He took out cupcake packs. Four of them. "Let's make a party."

"Brian!" Princess looked shocked. "Since when does your mom let you eat junk food?"

"They're good," said Brian.

Melody and I exchanged glances. Oh, no. Brian was still trading at school. I had to talk to him about that. Later, in private.

"How about we eat cupcakes this time?" I

said. "But after this, Brian's contribution will be cheering us on. And the club will cook only food that's good for you."

"I make the rules," said Kate. "But that's an okay one. There are only four packs, though. And there are five of us."

"I have to go anyway," said Princess.

"What?" said Kate. "We always stay for at least an hour."

"I forgot I have to be somewhere." Princess waved. "Bye."

"Wait," said Kate. "We have to figure out who's bringing what to my house on Monday. My recipe is rotini with meatballs. It's the hardest one because I'm in charge of the club."

"I'll bring the rotini," said Princess. "Bye."

Kate scowled as she watched Princess go out the door. "You might have a case soon, Sly."

I wanted to know more. But that scowl put me off. Kate was no fun when she was in a bad mood.

The Start

On Monday the cooking club met at Kate's house. That was because Kate's mother was the first parent to agree to this whole idea. Kate's mother agreed to just about anything. And she had persuaded the rest of our parents to give it a try.

Brian came with me. He was the club mascot, after all.

I brought ground beef. Melody brought canned tomatoes. Princess brought rotini. And Kate provided all the rest.

Except what Princess actually took out of her bag was not rotini. It was a sack of rice.

"Rice?" said Kate. "What can we do with rice?"

"Oops," said Princess. "They both start with *R*. I got confused."

"How could you get confused?" said Kate. "Your father is from Italy."

"Oh, well. My mother says pasta dishes taste

just as good with rice."

"Your mother's wrong," said Kate. "She's not from Italy."

What had gotten into Kate? First Brian's mother, now Princess's mother. Mother insults were bad news. If Kate said anything mean about my mother, I'd quit the club. After the linguine-with-pesto day.

"Good cooks are flexible," said Melody. "That's what my mother says."

"We could even make the rice Chinese-style," I said.

"I love Chinese food," said Princess.

"You're ganging up on me," said Kate. "All except Brian."

"I like rice," said Brian.

"Okay, okay," said Kate. "We'll make rice and meatballs. But not Chinese-style. This is an Italian cooking club. Everybody smile. We have to practice for the TV cameras."

Rice with meatballs wasn't half bad.

I was the last one out the door.

Kate stopped me. "Do you think Princess did it on purpose?"

"Did what?"

"Rice instead of rotini."

"No."

"Well, if she did, you've got a case."

New Additions

The cooking club skipped Tuesday because of Melody's ballet lesson. That was all right. My mother missed me at dinner on Monday, anyway. So she was glad on Tuesday.

On Wednesday we met at Melody's house. I brought olive oil. Kate brought garlic. Princess brought spaghetti. And Melody had everything else.

Before we got started, the doorbell rang.

"Are you expecting someone?" Kate asked Melody.

Melody shook her head.

"Well, whoever it is, make them go away," said Kate. "This is cooking club time."

We followed Melody to the door.

"Hi." Jack stood with a soccer ball under his arm. Another guy stood behind him. He had a soccer ball too. "We came to be tasters," said Jack.

Melody smiled big. She'd been smiling a lot at Jack lately.

"How did you find out about my cooking club?" asked Kate.

"Brian told me."

Brian clapped. "We played shuffleboard yesterday. I brought the pucks."

"Who's that?" asked Princess. She smiled at the other guy.

"My cousin Noah. He's staying with me for a while."

"Oh," said Kate.

"Well, come in," said Melody. "We have plenty."

"Hey, this is my club," said Kate. "I decide."

"It's my house," said Melody.

Kate opened her mouth. Then shut it. Then opened it. Then shut it. She reminded me of Jack's fish. She turned to the boys. "Tasters are an okay addition. Come in, Jack. And Noah."

We went back into the kitchen.

"What's that?" Kate pointed at the spaghetti box. "It's brown."

The spaghetti showed through the cellophane window of the box. Kate was right. Brown spaghetti.

Melody read the label. "Brown rice spaghetti."

"You brought rice again," said Kate. "Are you trying to make trouble, Princess?"

"It's spaghetti," said Princess. "It's just made from rice."

"What is it, Chinese spaghetti?" Kate glared at Princess.

"It's an experiment," said Princess. "It's good for you."

Kate put her fists on her hips and stared at me.

I could feel a case coming on.

"We said we'd make food that's good for you," said Melody.

Kate kept staring at me.

Yup, there was definitely a case coming on.

"I like rice," said Brian.

"I like everything," said Jack.

Noah didn't talk.

"Well, I guess we'll have to try it," said Kate.

Brown spaghetti turned out to taste better

than it looked. But it didn't taste normal.

"Listen," said Princess. "No one else has to bring anything tomorrow. I'll get all the ingredients, since I messed up."

Kate brightened. "That's fair."

It wasn't really fair. But Princess seemed to want to do it.

The Rest of the Week

On Thursday we met at Princess's house. It felt funny coming empty-handed.

"We're going to have a treat today," Princess announced. "Chocolate fondue."

"What's that?" said Brian.

"Fruit dipped in melted chocolate."

"That's not Italian," said Kate. "You were supposed to make macaroni. All our recipes are pasta."

"Pasta schmasta," said Jack.

"I get it," said Brian. "That means fruit's better than pasta, right?"

"Right," said Princess.

"And anything chocolate is good," said Melody.

"And anything fruit." I grinned.

Noah didn't talk.

Princess had us wash strawberries and cut up bananas and apples. She made Jack and Noah set the table.

I cut the apples into wedges.

Jack ate the cores.

"Ew," said Princess. "That's gross."

Jack stuffed two in his mouth at once.

Princess's eyes got huge.

Jack laughed so hard, he spit apple everywhere.

"You better not do that on TV," said Kate. "And you better clean it up, or I'll go find Princess's mother and tell on you."

Jack smirked. But he mopped the floor.

On Friday we met at my house. Kate brought linguine. Melody brought basil. I made sure we had the rest, because Princess couldn't come.

We ate well.

And Jack behaved. He hated mopping floors.

Noah behaved too, of course. I wondered if he knew how to misbehave.

Afterward Kate said, "If you boys are going to keep coming, you have to bring ingredients."

"Sure," said Jack. "I'll bring whatever's in the fridge at home."

"That's not how recipes work," said Kate.

"Take it or leave it," said Jack.

Melody looked at Kate with pleading eyes.

"Well . . ." said Kate. "I suppose that could work if you bring appetizers."

"Are pickles appetizers?" asked Jack.

"Pickles?" Kate wrinkled her nose.

"We can arrange them cute on a plate," said Melody

"I've got peanut butter too," said Jack.

"Peanut butter?" yelped Kate.

"Appetizers don't have to match the meal," I said. "They just have to taste good. And who doesn't like peanut butter?"

"All right, all right," said Kate. "But, Jack, you better not make trouble like Princess."

Trouble or no trouble, ending the week with a fruit fest and then linguine with pesto was perfect.

I liked cooking club.

A Case All Along

It was a chilly Saturday morning. Brian worked on his project. He was printing MASCOOK on an old T-shirt. He explained to me about the *ook* family: *look, book, hook, cook.* He really was smart.

He was happy.

But I was restless. Then I remembered.

"Hey, Brian. You have to stop trading your toys for junk food."

"Why?"

"First of all, you love your toys."

"I trade yours. And Melody's. They're not as good as mine."

I almost laughed. "And, worse, it's sneaking behind your mother's back. You can't do that."

"Okay."

Okay? Just like that? "Promise?"

"Yes."

Now what? I paced.

What I needed was a new case. It was time to advertise. I took out my sign. I scratched Taxi up and down her back while I looked at it.

Taxi had asked for extra love lately. My mother said the T-shirt episode was traumatic for her. It turns out cats hate clothes.

Taxi seemed to have forgiven us, though. She purred loud. I fed her the last fishy cookie I had.

This sign wasn't bad. But it wasn't good

either. And I had new poster board now. Maybe I could make a better one.

Knock knock.

I opened the door.

"I need to hire you," said Kate. She doesn't beat around the bush.

"Magic," said Brian.

"My case isn't about magic," said Kate.

"He means my sign," I said. "It works without being seen."

"Are you nuts?" asked Kate. No, she sure doesn't beat around the bush.

I sniffed indignantly. "What's the case?"

"Princess."

I knew this was coming. And I had already decided how to handle it. After all, Princess was my friend too. "Princess is a case?" I asked.

"Yes."

"Since when?" I asked.

"All along," said Kate. "Since she said 'Oh, no.'"

"When did she say 'Oh, no'?"

"When I started the club. Her attitude stinks. Something's cooking with her, all right."

Brian laughed. "I get it."

"What?" said Kate.

I grinned. "Did you hear what you just said?"

Kate looked at me. She gave a little smile of surprise. Then she frowned. "The real truth is just the opposite. Nothing's cooking with her. Princess is ruining the cooking club. And I want you to stop her. You're hired."

What Sleuths Do

"Sleuths don't stop people," I said. "Sleuths find out who's doing what. And why."

"Then find out why Princess wants to ruin my club," said Kate. "And I'll stop her."

"How do you know she wants to ruin it?"

"She brought rice instead of rotini," said Kate.

"That was a mistake."

"She brought brown spaghetti," said Kate.

"That was an experiment."

"She made chocolate fondue with fruit."

"That was delicious," I said.

"You're making trouble," said Kate. "Just like Princess. Are you going to help me or not?"

"I don't think there's a case here, Kate."

"Yes there is. Princess didn't even come to the club on Friday. Then, this morning, I invited her over for pancakes."

"I love pancakes," said Brian.

"Why did you invite her?" I asked.

"Do I need a reason?"

"I just thought it might be something special."

"Well, it wasn't special," said Kate. "It was ordinary. And she said no."

"I wouldn't say no," said Brian. He pulled

his MASCOOK T-shirt on over his sweater.

Kate's mother made amazing pancakes. "Did you tell her your mother adds fresh fruit?"

"Yes."

"Oh," I said. I wondered why Kate hadn't invited me. I love fresh fruit.

"See?" Kate's voice got quiet. "See, Sly? Princess is up to something."

It did seem to add up. "Maybe there's a grain of truth in what you're saying."

"And I haven't told you the worst yet." Kate blinked hard. Her voice got even quieter. "Princess said she can't stay in the club. And after I made it Italian food, just for her. Just because her father's from Italy. Just so she'd feel welcome, being the new kid in school and all. And now she won't even be in it."

"Did she say why not?"

"No. But I know," said Kate.

"You think she wants to ruin the club," I said. "You told me."

"And I know why."

"Really? Then you don't need me."

"Yes I do. She wants to ruin it because she hates me." Kate's voice cracked. She wiped her nose with the back of her hand. "You have to find out why she hates me. Is that something a sleuth can do?"

I stepped close to her. Brian came close too. Even Taxi came close.

No one likes being hated. Taxi understood that. She'd want me to take this case. Probably any cat would.

"Sure, Kate. Definitely."

Kate sniffled. "That's a cute T-shirt," she said to Brian.

Princess's Kitchen

I stood outside Princess's house. The sidewalk was empty. I shifted from foot to foot. I scratched my neck. And ribs. And bottom.

How did you ask someone if they hated someone else?

And if they said yes, how did you convince them not to?

Maybe I shouldn't have taken this case.

"Are you casing the joint?"

I spun around.

Jack and Noah. They had appeared from nowhere.

"How did you get here? A second ago there was no one on the street."

"Tricks," said Jack.

Noah didn't talk.

"Go away," I said. "I'm on a case."

"Then I was right! You are casing the joint." Jack gave Noah the high five. "We'll help."

"I don't need help."

"Hello!" Princess stood at her door. "Did you come over to see me?" Her eyes were on Noah. "Come in."

Jack walked ahead of us. "Got any chocolate fondue left?"

"No. But we have carrot sticks. And veggie dip."

"I like everything," said Jack.

Princess opened the fridge. She put carrot sticks on a tray. And veggie dip. She added chunks of cheese. And cut-up cauliflower.

This looked like a health food tray. Was her mother friends with Brian's mother?

Then it hit me. None of the food on that tray was Italian. And none of the food Princess had contributed to the cooking club so far was Italian.

And when Kate had called Princess Italian, Princess had said no—she was American.

Maybe it was odd enough being the new kid at school. Maybe Princess didn't want to be known as the Italian kid too. Maybe Kate had picked exactly the wrong kind of cooking to welcome Princess with.

I didn't like making Princess feel odd. But I had to help Kate. "Is that Italian cheese?" I asked softly.

"Of course." Princess looked proud. "We buy tons of Italian cheese. It's great."

So much for that idea. I was back at square one. Poor Kate. I might never figure this case out.

"Got any crackers?" asked Jack. "For the cheese."

Jack sure was rude. It was true, though: Crackers went great with cheese.

Princess opened a cupboard. She put a box on the tray. Yellow, with black specks. I read the label. Peppery corn crackers.

"Want to sit in the sunroom? Come on." Princess picked up the tray.

Noah jumped in front of her. He grabbed the edges of the tray.

Princess struggled to hold on.

"Let go," said Noah at last. So he could talk, after all.

"He wants to carry it for you," said Jack.

"Oh." Princess let go. "Oh. Thanks."

Noah carried the tray out to the sunroom.

I lingered in the kitchen. The cupboard was still open. Cornmeal. Rice flour. Millet. Quinoa.

Wasn't millet bird food?

And what on earth was quinoa?

Orange Grove

At the back of a shelf was a box of ordinary crackers. I took them out to the sunroom.

Wow. Princess's sunroom was way better than my porch. It was filled with trees in giant pots.

"What're those?" Jack pointed to the round, green fruits.

"Oranges."

I recognized them now. The trees were loaded with them. And some were turning color.

Jack whistled. "An orange grove. Right here in your house."

"My father grew oranges as a boy," said Princess.

"Back in Italy," I said helpfully.

"Sicily," said Princess.

"Sicily is part of Italy," I said.

"Not according to my father." Princess smiled. "He says Sicily is its own place. Anyway, he still grows oranges. Wherever we live. We bought this house because of the big sunroom."

"You should have served the cooking club oranges instead of apples," said Jack.

"I don't like orange with chocolate. Besides, they aren't ripe yet."

I saw my opening. "Talking about eating," I said, "let's eat."

I took a little of everything.

Jack and Noah heaped their plates with a lot of everything.

Princess took a little of everything. Except the crackers I brought out. The ordinary ones.

"Want a cracker, Princess?" I pushed the box toward her.

"No thanks."

I wasn't surprised.

"This is like a party," I said. "Maybe I should call Kate. What do you think, Princess?"

"Sure," said Princess.

I wasn't surprised at that either.

"And Melody," said Jack.

"Actually," I said, "I just remembered. Kate

and Melody are busy right now." I stuffed a cracker and cheese in my mouth. Princess was right: Italian cheese is great.

The Internet

I went into our family room. I sat down at the computer.

Millet is yellow grain from Africa and Asia. I was right: It is bird food. But it's also people food.

Quinoa is a grain from Peru. You say it "keen-wah." It has a nutty flavor.

I learned this from a website about food allergies. People who can't eat wheat eat these other grains. And rice too. And corn.

Princess brought rice instead of rotini. She brought brown spaghetti made from rice instead of regular spaghetti. She served fruit and chocolate instead of macaroni and cheese.

And when she filled her plate in her sunroom, she ate corn crackers but not regular crackers.

I telephoned Princess.

"Hello."

"Hi, Princess. Do you hate Italian food?"

"No, I like it."

It was tough to ask, but I had to: "Do you hate Kate?"

"No, I like her."

"Do you hate birthday parties?"

"Well, parts of them. But I go if I'm invited. Are you having one?"

"No. Is it the birthday-cake part you hate?"

"Yes," said Princess.

"Are you allergic to wheat?"

Princess made a loud sigh. "You figured it out. I knew I should have quit the club right away. But I was afraid I'd have no one to play with. Kate's recipes are awful. Wheat makes me feel yucky."

"Why keep it a secret?" I said. "Lots of people have allergies."

"Yeah. But kids think you're sickly if you tell them," said Princess. "I know. They treat me different once they find out. So I keep it to myself."

"Well, I think you should tell your friends," I said. "Otherwise they get confused by what you do."

"You mean Kate?"

"And Melody. And Brian too. Even Jack and Noah. We're all your friends, Princess."

Back to Cheerleading

Princess told Kate she was allergic to wheat. So Kate said the cooking club could change. No more pasta.

But Princess said she really wanted to be a cheerleader. She said cheerleaders get on TV too.

Kate said it wasn't the same thing. Who

ever heard of a cheerleading channel? But her ankle feels okay now, and she really likes Princess. She said managing the cooking club was a lot of trouble, anyway. Besides, her mother wanted her to go back to cheerleading for the exercise. Kate's mother is on a health kick. She has been for months.

We're a cheerleading squad again.

Kate wanted to celebrate that Princess didn't hate her. So she invited Princess and Melody and me to a sleepover.

Brian was sad because he had no place to wear his MASCOOK T-shirt. But Kate told him he could wear it to basketball games. So he got happy again.

Jack was sad because he liked being a taster. Kate didn't say anything to that. After all, what could she say?

And all our parents were glad to have us back for family meals.

So the mystery of Princess was solved. And

it was all about food. Wow. Kate had been right when she said something was cooking with Princess. Words are funny like that. They mean so many things. Ha, ha.

Case #3:
Sly and Something Seedy

The Smell of Apples

Princess stood at my living room window. "January is cold here."

"This is worse than usual," I said.

"It snows too much," said Princess.

"I like it, though," said Melody. "It makes ice-skating fun."

Melody is good at ice-skating.

"I love ice-skating," said Brian.

Brian is bad at ice-skating.

"What about you?" asked Princess. "Do you skate, Sly?"

"Not much. I like it inside. Nice and warm."

"I'd like something warm right now," said

Princess. "Something to make us feel cozy."

"Let's bake apples," I said.

We trooped into the kitchen.

Melody and I washed apples.

"I'll cut the cores out," said Princess. "It's important to get rid of all the seeds."

So Princess cut out the cores.

Brian filled the holes: sugar, cinnamon, and a pat of butter.

We put them in the oven.

"We have apple cider too," I said.

"Let's heat it," said Melody. "Hot cider is best."

"With cinnamon sticks and cloves," said Princess.

So we made spicy hot cider.

"Apple party," said Brian. "Apple, apple, apple party."

I love all fruit. But apples are my favorite. They smell great. My father says I'm the apple of his eye.

Cooking together like this made me miss the old cooking club.

We went back into the living room. We sipped our cider and waited for the apples to bake soft.

I smiled at Brian and Melody and Princess. It was funny. Earlier this morning, I had taken out my sleuth sign. I was bored. I was going to put it up.

Brian came over and added more hearts to it. But we never put it up because then Melody and Princess came.

And look what a nice morning this was turning out to be. Who needed sleuthing?

Seedy

Thud. The noise came from the porch door. *Thud, thud.*

"Jack!" screamed Brian.

Jack would have to be crazy to be kicking his soccer ball around in this snow.

I opened the door.

A snow-coated ball sailed past me. It hit the inside wall.

Jack was crazy.

And his jacket was covered with snow and mud. "Jack, you look like a bum. You look seedy."

"I have a case for you," said Jack.

"Magic magic magic," sang Brian.

I had to admit it. That sign sure seemed magic.

I looked at the snowball mess. "My mother

won't like that." I got the mop and handed it to Jack.

Jack groaned. But he cleaned up the puddle.

Princess peeked in. "Hi, Jack." She gave a quick wave and disappeared into the kitchen.

Jack sniffed the air. "Apple pie?"

"Cider and baked apples," I said.

"Come have some," said Melody. She stood beside me now. Melody seemed to like feeding Jack.

"Sure."

"Take off your dirty jacket," I said.

Jack took off his jacket.

"What's your case?" I asked.

"Shhh," said Jack. "I can't tell you now."

"Then why did you come over?" I whispered.

"I'll tell you later," Jack whispered back.

"You can come in now," called Princess.

What was she talking about?

We went into the kitchen.

Our mess was gone. Princess had wiped the

counter clean. She'd thrown the apple cores in the compost bin.

Before I could thank her, the phone rang.

"Hello?"

"Hello, Sly. This is Mrs. Monti. I need to talk with Princess a minute."

"Sure." I handed the phone to Princess. "Your mother," I mouthed.

"Hi, Mamma." Princess nodded. "Now?" Princess turned her back to us. "All right. . . . Okay. . . . Bye." She hung up and turned to us. "I have to go. My mother needs me to pick up cheese for her."

"Can't you wait till after the baked apples?" I asked.

"She's in the middle of cooking. Sorry."

I waved my arm around the kitchen. "Thanks, but you didn't have to do all that work yourself," I said.

"I didn't mind. And see? Everything's nice and safe now."

Safe? "Is something wrong, Princess?"

"I just have to hurry. Bye." Princess pulled on her jacket and left.

Thief

"Good," said Jack. "Now I can tell you about my case."

"You mean you couldn't tell with Princess here?"

"Nope."

This was interesting.

I went to the drawer and got my special pencil. And special pad of paper. These are tools of the trade. I sat on the couch. "Give me the details," I said. That's sleuth talk.

"You have to catch a thief."

I put away the paper and pencil. "Sleuths aren't the police."

"I don't mean you have to put him in jail.

Just find out who he is. Then I can stop him."

"Have you told your parents?" asked Melody.

"Hey," I said. "I'm the one who asks questions."

"You already put away your paper and pencil," said Melody.

"That doesn't matter," I said.

"Why not?" said Melody.

I couldn't think of a reason. "Because."

"You're acting like Kate," said Melody.

That hurt. I turned to Jack. "Well? Are you going to answer Melody's question?"

"No," said Jack.

"No, you're not going to answer or no, you didn't tell your parents?" I asked.

"You're the first one I've told," said Jack.

"And the second and the third," said Brian.

"What?" said Jack.

"You told Melody and me too. First, second, third," said Brian. "If you tell someone else, that will be fourth. After that, fifth. Like fingers."

Jack looked blankly at Brian.

"Why didn't you tell your parents?" I asked.

"It's the sort of thing only you would understand."

Jack sometimes said smart things, even if he was wacky.

"Tell me more."

"It's about fruit."

"Someone's stealing your fruit?" I asked.

"Sort of," said Jack.

"Sort of ?" asked Melody.

"It's complicated," said Jack. "Are the baked apples ready?"

Oranges

We sat at the table. Steam came out of the baked apples.

"Careful, Brian," I said. "Blow first."

Brian blew on his apple. He put a spoonful in his mouth. "Ow!"

"Blow more."

"So," said Melody, "tell us the details, Jack."

That was one of my sleuth lines. I kicked Melody under the table.

"Ow," said Melody.

"Blow first," said Brian.

"That's not why I said 'Ow,'" said Melody. "I haven't even taken a bite yet." She glared at me.

"Go ahead, Jack," I said. "Talk."

"For the last three days I've gone to Princess's house—"

"What?" said Melody. Her face fell.

"—to talk with Mr. Monti—"

"Oh," breathed Melody.

"—and he chose the right orange for me from his sunroom and gave it to me—"

"Why were you talking to Mr. Monti?" asked Melody. "And what do you mean, he chose an orange for you? Why didn't you choose one yourself?"

Those were the obvious questions. I kicked Melody under the table again.

"Ow!"

I felt bad. It wasn't nice to kick. But I was the sleuth. What was the matter with Melody? In the future I would question my client in private. For now, though, I was stuck.

"Well?" I said.

"I like to meet Mr. Monti as he gets home from work," said Jack. "We talk."

97

"Talk about what?"

Jack stuffed his mouth with baked apple.

"Are you trying to avoid answering?" I asked.

"Blllmgr," mumbled Jack.

"Stop eating long enough to answer."

"Well . . ." Jack looked down. "I can't tell you."

I frowned. "Jack, this is dumb. Why can't you tell us something so simple?"

"Because then you'll know why I want the oranges. And it's a secret."

"What do you mean?" said Melody. "There's only one reason to want oranges. To eat them."

"That's not my reason," said Jack. He stuffed his mouth with baked apple.

Melody and Brian and I waited for Jack to say more.

"Tell us," said Brian at last.

"No. But you have to believe me: It's a good

reason. Anyway, I put the orange in my backpack. All three times. But when I got home, it was gone."

"Gone," said Brian sadly. "All gone."

"Right." Jack took another bite. "I never even got the chance to use the orange. Someone stole it from me. Every time. Find out who, Sly."

Use the orange? How does someone use an orange?

"Did you check your backpack the instant you got home?"

"Of course," said Jack. "And it was gone."

"Did you stop anywhere on your way home?"

"Nope."

"Did you bump into anyone?"

"Nope."

"Does your backpack have holes?"

"I already thought of that." Jack held his chin up. "None of them are big enough for an orange to fall through."

This seemed like an easy problem to solve. "Next time Mr. Monti gives you an orange, hold it in your hand all the way home."

"But then Princess will see. She always comes out to say good-bye when I leave."

One missing orange, that was an annoyance. Two missing oranges, that was a pity. But three missing oranges? That was a pattern.

I looked out the window at the clean, white snow. I got an idea. It was unlikely. But a good sleuth checks every possibility. "Stay here. All of you. I'll be back."

Snow

I stood outside Princess's house.

Should I take Jack's case? Princess was my friend. I didn't want to spy on my friend's house.

But Jack was really upset.

A little investigation couldn't hurt.

Princess's front walk had not yet been shoveled. Good. There were many sets of footprints in the snow. Some of them were on top of others. So it was hard to be sure how many.

There were no footprints in the snow on the front grass.

I looked along one side of Princess's yard. Then I looked along the other side.

There were no footprints in the snow on the side grass.

I walked around the block to the house behind Princess's. It was big and blue. I had no idea who lived there.

It is not a good idea to walk through the yard of strangers. They might get mad. Or they might get afraid. They could call the police.

I rang the doorbell.

A man answered. He leaned on a cane. "What can I do for you, little lady?"

"Could I please go in your backyard? I want

to look at the rear of my friend's house. She lives behind you."

"She's your friend, huh? So why don't you just walk around the side of her house to look at the rear?"

"I don't want anyone in her house to see me."

"That sounds suspicious," said the man.

"I'm a sleuth," I said. "I run a detective agency. So the things I do sound suspicious. But they're not really."

The man pursed his lips. "What's your name?"

"Sly."

Now he pulled on his earlobe. "What's your real name?"

"Sylvia."

"I had a cat named Sylvia once. Okay." He shut the door.

Okay? Did he mean it was okay for me to go in his yard?

My father laughs at the funny things kids say. But adults say funny things too.

I ran around to the back of his yard. I peeked into Princess's yard.

There were no footprints in Princess's back-yard.

Misting

I went home. Jack and Brian and Melody were playing dominoes in the porch.

"Did you find out who the thief is already?" asked Jack.

"No. Come with me."

"Can I come too?" asked Brian.

"There might be sleuthing to do. Stay with Melody."

Melody looked crushed. I knew she wanted to come. But then she perked up. "We can go ice-skating."

"I love ice-skating," said Brian.

Melody and Brian left through the porch door.

Jack and I went out the front door.

"Where are we going?" asked Jack.

"To Princess's. You went there yesterday, right?"

"I told you. After school Noah and I kicked around the soccer ball a while. Then we split and I went to talk to Mr. Monti."

"Was it snowing when you left Princess's house?" I asked.

"No. It had already stopped.

"Good," I said.

"Good? Sometimes you don't make sense, Sly." Jack kicked his soccer ball into a mound of snow. Then into another. Then into another.

I led the way up Princess's front walk. Jack stashed his ball beside the door. I rang the bell.

Princess's father answered. He was tall. And

he had a long mustache. And a lot of spiky hair. He looked sort of like an upside-down broom.

"Hello, Mr. Monti," I said. "Is Princess home?"

"Come in, come in." Mr. Monti smiled big. He stepped aside so we could pass.

"Hello." Princess came running to the door. She held a bucket. "Oh, it's you. I thought it was Noah." She handed me the bucket. "It's my job to do the trees. You're just in time to help."

She got another bucket for Jack. And she took one too. She led us to her front yard. "Fill your buckets with snow."

We filled our buckets with snow.

I had no idea what was going on. But this was fun.

We followed Princess back inside.

She dumped the snow into a pot. She heated it on the stove. The snow melted.

Cooking snow was batty. But it was still fun.

Next she filled plastic bottles with the melted snow. The bottles had little hoses on them. And a squirter at the end.

We went into the sunroom armed with our squirter bottles. Princess squirted an orange tree up near the top.

Jack walked over to a pot. He put his finger in the dirt. He squirted the dirt.

"Stop," said Princess.

"But it's dry. And, hey, you don't know so

much, Princess. Plants drink through their roots. Not their leaves."

Princess laughed. "We're not watering. We're misting. In winter we water once a week. But we mist every day. Like this." She squirted high in a tree. "Try to get the whole tree. Top to bottom."

"What good does misting do?" asked Jack.

"They need humidity," said Princess.

"Why use melted snow?" asked Jack.

"There's salt in tap water. It's bad for the trees."

"What happens when there's no snow?" asked Jack.

He sure was full of questions.

"We use distilled water. But after we finish misting today, we can fill lots of buckets with snow. That way we'll have enough for the whole week."

I looked at Jack.

But he didn't have any more questions.

We misted all those trees.

Then we stood in a little group. We admired our work.

I finally saw my chance. "Hey, Princess, did anyone visit your house last night?"

"No. My father went out and got us a video. Our whole family likes to curl up together on the couch when it snows."

"What about this morning?"

"What?"

"Did anyone visit your house this morning?"

Princess gave me a cockeyed smile. "You two." She laughed.

"Besides us," I said.

"No. What's this all about?"

"Just asking."

Lunch

"Wait here," said Princess. She left us in the sunroom.

Jack looked over his shoulder. "Have you got any leads on my case?" he whispered.

"Maybe."

Princess came back. "Want to stay for lunch?"

"Sure," said Jack.

"Thanks," I said.

"Do you like gorgonzola?" asked Princess.

"What's gorgonzola?" I asked.

"It's smelly cheese."

"How smelly?" asked Jack.

"Very."

"Do you like it?" I asked.

"I love it," said Princess.

"I'll try it," I said.

"The smellier, the better," said Jack.

We sat at the table with Princess's mother and father and her big sister, Angel.

We ate polenta with gorgonzola. It was really corn mush with blue cheese. But they called it polenta with gorgonzola.

It was fabulous.

Afterward Mr. Monti brought out a bowl of oranges.

Jack threw me a quick look.

"Are those from your trees?" I asked Mr. Monti.

"Of course," said Mr. Monti. "Aren't they beautiful?"

"Yes."

Mr. Monti and Jack exchanged glances.

Princess grabbed the bowl. She took two oranges and passed the bowl. Away from Jack.

"Hey, I want one," said Jack.

"I know," said Princess. "I'll fix it for you."

"I don't want you to," said Jack.

"I've seen you eat apple cores. You'll probably just eat the orange whole too," said Princess.

"So you're the one," said Angel. "I heard all about you. That's gross."

"Gross and dangerous," said Princess. "I already told you that, Jack."

Dangerous?

Princess peeled an orange.

"It's red," I yelped.

"Blood oranges," said Princess.

"Aw, cool," said Jack. "Blood."

"That's just the name. Because the flesh is red." Princess divided the orange into sections. She popped the seeds out onto her plate. She gave the seedless sections to Jack.

"Want an orange?" Princess asked me.

I didn't like the idea of eating blood-

colored fruit. "Next time," I said.

"I'll take Sly's orange," said Jack. "And don't peel it."

"That's okay. I'll save one for Sly." Princess rolled an orange in her hands. "I'll put it with the oranges for Noah." She put my orange into a bowl on the shelf.

Nutrition

Jack and I walked back to my house.

"Princess is saving oranges for Noah," Jack said. He sounded worried.

"What's wrong with that?" I said.

"One of them was really big. Perfect. I wanted it. Maybe Princess is saving it for him because . . . "

"Because what?"

"Nothing. You better take my case."

"Where is Noah today?" I asked.

"He's working on a school project. You know, the nutrition one. His partner is Princess."

"Oh." Now it made sense. "That's why Princess thought it was Noah at the door. That's why she's saving him oranges. So he can have a snack when he comes over to finish the project."

"I hope you're right," said Jack. He kicked his soccer ball. He ran after it and dribbled it back.

"I worked with Kate," I said. "We finished already. On potassium. Bananas are full of potassium. What's your project on?"

Jack jumped in front of me. He put his hands up like claws. "Blood!"

I walked past him. "You can't do a nutrition project on blood."

"Iron, really," said Jack. "It's in bloody meat."

"Not just meat," I said. "Spinach too. And most dark green vegetables."

"Yeah, but meat has more. Paul and I wrote

all about meat. Bloody meat." Jack tilted his head. "I wonder if those blood oranges have iron."

"Oranges don't have iron."

"You don't know everything, Sly."

That was true. But I know a lot about fruit. The only fruit that has a lot of iron is raisins.

I didn't feel like arguing with Jack, though. I had other things on my mind. "What's Noah and Princess's project on?" I asked.

"Poisons," said Jack.

"Poisons!"

"Noah has all the luck. He gets to write about poisons in our food. But blood is almost as good."

Someone in the Family

Jack stopped in front of his house. "You have to work harder, Sly."

"What do you mean?" I said.

"You've been on the case since this morning. And you haven't solved anything yet." He dribbled his soccer ball in a circle around me.

"Jack, I never agreed to take your case. And I won't."

"What? Why not?"

"There is no case."

"What?"

"There's no thief," I said. "Or not a thief thief."

"What's a thief thief?"

"Someone who sneaks in and steals. No one like that stole oranges from your backpack."

"How do you know?" asked Jack.

"A thief thief would have left footprints. But there were no footprints in the snow around

Princess's house this morning. The only footprints were on the front walk."

"How do you know?" asked Jack.

"It's my job."

"That doesn't prove anything," said Jack. "A tricky thief could have used the front walk."

"True." I stuck my hands deep in my pockets and leaned into the wind. Sleuths do that. "But Princess said no one had visited them except us. The footprints on their front walk were from their family."

Jack picked at a muddy spot on his jacket.

"You mean someone in Princess's family robbed me?"

"Yup."

"I was afraid of that," said Jack. "It's Princess, isn't it?"

"I think so."

"I knew it." Jack looked like he might cry. "She's against me."

"What are you talking about?"

Jack kicked the snow.

"Come on, Jack."

"I can't explain without telling you my secret."

"Listen, Jack. Sleuths are good at keeping secrets. So long as it doesn't hurt anyone."

Jack screwed up his mouth. "Okay, but you have to swear. You absolutely can't tell Princess. Because then she'll tell Noah."

"This is getting complicated," I said. "But I swear. So, why do you want oranges?"

"For soccer."

"You want to kick oranges?"

"No. I'll juggle them with my feet. Like Pelé. He's a famous player. People say he got good by juggling grapefruits. My feet are smaller. So oranges are better. Mr. Monti picks oranges that are exactly right."

"Mr. Monti knows what you want to use them for?"

"Mr. Monti knows everything about soccer. I can ask him anything and he talks and talks and talks."

"Why don't you want Noah to know?" I asked.

"He's already good at soccer. Too good. What if he sticks around till spring? What if he makes the team and I don't?"

"Oh," I said. I sympathized. Jack worked even harder at soccer than I worked at baseball. And I love baseball.

"Now I'll never get better at soccer." Jack's voice was sad. He dribbled his soccer ball around me again. "Why? Why would Princess take my oranges?"

"I'm not entirely sure it's Princess."

"Why would anyone take my oranges?" Jack kicked the ball against a tree. "Someone is being mean to me. Find out who, Sly."

Decision

Did I want to take Jack's case?

Jack's case was about oranges. I love fruit. So this case was fun.

But Taxi had no interest in fruit. I couldn't take a case Taxi wouldn't care about.

I went home and into our garage. That's where we keep Taxi's little house. It's really a picnic cooler. Brian had the idea. He turned it upside down and my mother cut a hole in it so Taxi can get in and out. Taxi loves it.

"Hey, Taxi."

Taxi came out of her cooler. She rubbed against my legs.

I squatted to pet her. "Do you even know what an orange is?"

Taxi purred and pressed harder against my legs.

I pet her more.

She bumped her head into me hard. I fell onto my bottom on the cold garage floor.

Taxi jumped in my lap. Then she climbed to my shoulder. Like she used to do when she was a kitten.

"Hey, I'm not a tree."

Taxi purred more.

I laughed. That was it. This case wasn't just about oranges. It was about orange trees too. Taxi loved to climb trees. She'd care about a tree case. Probably any cat would.

Good. Because this case had hooked me. I was almost sure Princess was the culprit. The question was, why?

Hunches

In sleuthing it helps to make a list of what you know.

This is what I knew.

Jack went to Princess's house three days in a row to talk about soccer with Mr. Monti. Mr. Monti gave him an orange. Jack slipped it into his backpack.

When he got home, his orange was gone.

Always.

Maybe Princess was nabbing back the oranges that her father gave Jack. Maybe she didn't want Jack to have oranges.

But she gave him an orange at lunch. She even peeled it. And she seeded it. Seeds.

Princess had cored the apples this morning. She said it was important to get rid of the seeds.

And at lunch she and Angel talked about how gross it was that Jack ate apple cores.

Princess and Noah's project was on poisons in the foods we eat.

Fruit's my favorite food. I know a lot about apples. And I know a lot about apple seeds.

I went home and put a baked apple into a plastic container. I went back to Princess's house. I rang the doorbell.

"Hi, Sly. What's up?"

"I brought you a baked apple," I said.

"Thanks." Princess took the apple. "This is the third time we've seen each other today."

"I know." I couldn't think of what else to say. Finally, I blurted out, "Did you know that your father has been giving Jack oranges?"

"Yes," said Princess.

"Do you know why?"

"Is there a special reason?"

"Yes," I said. "But I can't tell you. Have you been stealing them back?"

"Yes," said Princess.

"Because you're afraid he'll eat the oranges whole, seeds and all, like he does apples?"

"Yes," said Princess.

"And you think he'll get poisoned?"

"Yes. With arsenic."

"But arsenic is in apple seeds," I said.

"Not only apple seeds" said Princess. "All kinds of fruit seeds."

"Why didn't you just tell Jack the seeds have poison?"

"I did. But Jack never listens." Princess shrugged. "What else could I do?"

No One Dies

Princess showed me her library book. She was right: Arsenic is in most fruit seeds. But we checked out another book. That's where we learned about the amount of arsenic in a seed. It's very little. You'd have to eat a barrel of seeds all at once to poison yourself. Even then, you would probably only vomit.

Princess was relieved.

Jack was happy to learn that no one was being mean to him. Princess had been protecting him. He went to Princess's house and thanked her.

Then he got into a conversation with Mr. Monti about the orange trees. And before you knew it, Jack had a job. From now on Jack has to go to Mr. Monti's house every weekend. He'll help with the trees. He's going to learn how to fertilize them. And when to repot them. How to prune the tips. And how to do root cuttings.

Mr. Monti will pay him in oranges. That's because Mr. Monti loves soccer as much as Jack does. He said he'll teach Jack how to juggle good. Serious practice will use up lots of oranges. But Mr. Monti thinks Jack has promise. He said Jack's worth the oranges.

Jack is going to give me half a dozen oranges as my payment for this case.

I don't really want bloody-looking oranges. But I'll find something to do with them.

And Jack is going to give Melody an orange every day. He's going to surprise her. An orange in her school cubby. An orange in her backpack. Oranges here and there. Then, when he's sure she likes them, he's going to tell her he was the secret giver. And he's going to invite her to the school Valentine's party.

He told me because of the hearts on my sleuth sign. He said they mean I know about romance. He wanted my opinion.

I don't know about romance. I know about sleuthing. I told him that.

This case was about seeds. And when Jack showed up this morning covered with snow and mud, he had looked seedy. My seedy case was solved. Ha.

These last three cases were all like that. They

were about food. And they had plays on words. The first was about fish, and there was something fishy in it. The second was about food allergies, and there was something cooking in it. And the third was about fruit, and there was something seedy in it.

Playing with words is something poets do.

Somehow all my cases wind up being poetic. I like that. Ha. These cases were food for thought, all right. Ha, ha.